The Future's Destiny

Steampunk OZ: Book 4

by Steve DeWinter

I0625855

Summary

There is no yellow brick road here. No emerald city. No lollipop guild. This is the Australis Penal Colony, a continent sized prison referred to the world over as the Outcast Zone. Built to contain the world's most dangerous criminals, OZ ended up the dumping ground for everything polite society deemed undesirable.

Book 4

Captured by the West Marshal, Dorothy has one chance to survive and is closer than ever to finding her father. Can Caleb be trusted to help her finish her quest?

This book is a work of fiction. References to real people, events, establishments, organization, or locales are intended only to provide a sense of authenticity, and are used fictitiously. All other characters, and all incidents and dialogue, are drawn from the author's imagination and are not to be construed as real.

Ramblin' Prose Publishing

Copyright © 2014 Steve DeWinter

All rights reserved. Used under authorization.

www.stevedw.com

eBook Edition
ISBN-10: 1-61978-038-0
ISBN-13: 978-1-61978-038-5

Paperback Edition
ISBN-10: 1-61978-039-9
ISBN-13: 978-1-61978-039-2

Chapter 1

High atop the Western Territories, in the dining hall of the tallest spire of the castle, Dorothy sat on the opposite end of the long banquet table from the West Marshal.

Servants were still placing platters of fresh fruit and ornately cut vegetables on the table between them.

The West Marshal plucked a grape off the platter in front of her and looked across the table at Dorothy. She popped the grape in her mouth. "I'm afraid we got off on the wrong foot. When we first met I was under the assumption that you killed my sister in order to take over as the East Marshal."

Dorothy started to speak but the West Marshal raised a finger and cut her off. "Let me finish. Now I see my assumption was all wrong and you have but one goal here in OZ. To find your father."

Dorothy sat up straighter in her chair. "That's all I ever wanted. I just happened to be in airship that crashed in OZ. I never intended to kill anyone."

The West Marshal stabbed at a cube of honeydew melon with a fork. "I see that now and believe we can help each other. You have something that I want and I have something that you want."

People had been saying this to Dorothy ever since she crashed in OZ and it was seldom true. It always meant they wanted something she could not give or something bad was about to happen to her. In this case, the opposite was true. There was nothing the West Marshal could offer her. "What could you possibly have that I want?"

The West Marshal pointed at Dorothy. "Take a look at your necklace."

She looked down and saw her necklace was glowing brightly through her clothing.

She looked back up at the West Marshal. "My father is here?"

The West Marshal shook her head and pulled at the leather strap around her own neck. She produced an equally brilliant glowing emerald heart necklace. "I have your father's necklace."

Dorothy stood up, knocking her chair over. "What have you done with my father!?"

The guards on either side of the room stepped toward her and drew their swords. The West Marshal held up a hand. "Wait!"

She looked back at Dorothy. "Please have a seat."

"No thanks. I'll stand."

The West Marshal nodded toward one of the guards. "I'm afraid I must insist. For your own safety."

The guard sheathed his sword and lifted the chair up. As Dorothy settled back into the chair he pushed it up against the table.

"What have you done with my father?" she said through clenched teeth.

The West Marshal slipped the necklace over her head and placed it on the table in front of her. "The last I heard, Nero had him."

Dorothy's heart sank. She had been so close. But without the necklace, she never knew it. She looked deeply into the West Marshal's eyes. "Can you help me get him back?"

The West Marshal smiled. "Yes I can. Nero has something you want. I have something Nero wants. And you have something I want. Three players. Three trades. We all get what we want."

"What do you want from me?"

"I want the East Marshal star. I will give you the necklace in exchange for it and you can use the necklace to get your father from Nero."

Dorothy clutched at her necklace. It felt warm from the glow. "I already have a necklace. Why do I need yours?"

"You silly little girl. You don't even know what you have. Nero wants both necklaces. Having only one is useless."

"Why does he want both of them?"

"That is hardly important, isn't it? All that should matter is giving him both necklaces will get your father back."

"How do I know I can trust you?"

A side door opened and everyone's attention turned to the door as Amanda and Caleb both entered the dining hall. Amanda was smiling one of her patented wicked smiles as she walked in carrying two bottles of clear liquid. Caleb refused to make eye contact with Dorothy as he shuffled in silently behind Amanda.

The West Marshal clasped her hands together. "You can trust me because we are going to toast to our new-found friendship."

Amanda handed each bottle to separate servants who walked to each end of the table and poured the liquid into glass goblets in front of both the West Marshal and Dorothy.

While they poured, the West Marshal looked across the table at her. "One of the most precious commodities in all of OZ is a clean glass of water..."

Dorothy interrupted her. "I know, I know. Nero has a whole fountain of it just for looking at."

The West Marshal laughed. "He was always one to flaunt his excess." She grabbed her goblet and held it aloft, letting some of the water slosh out over the lip. "To us, Dorothy. May this be the start of a long-enduring friendship."

Dorothy picked up her goblet and glanced over Caleb. He had apparently been watching her but quickly looked down at the floor as soon as she looked over at him.

She looked back at the West Marshal and held her goblet in the air. "To my father."

The West Marshal nodded her head. "To your father." She tilted the goblet to her lips and drank it all without stopping.

Dorothy placed the edge of the goblet on her lips and sipped at the water. It tasted cool and refreshing, just like water should.

The West Marshal looked at her over the spread of exotic foods on the table that was far more than just the two of them could ever hope to finish in one sitting. Just another example of flaunting your excess, Dorothy thought.

The West Marshal tilted her head to one side and showed Dorothy her own empty goblet. "The toast doesn't count unless you drink it all."

Dorothy took a deep breath and gulped down the rest of her water.

The West Marshal watched her intently as if waiting for something to happen.

Dorothy's throat constricted and she looked over at Caleb who continued to stare at the floor.

She looked back at the West Marshal who visibly relaxed and sat back in her chair.

Dorothy's heart pounded in her chest and her breathing increased in shallow spurts as she realized the water was most likely poisoned.

She looked at Caleb.

He glanced up at her and she could see his eyes glisten as he held back the tears. He silently mouthed the words "I'm sorry."

She looked back at the West Marshal who was smiling by now.

She had been tricked into drinking poison under the guise of friendship.

She clawed at her throat and started taking heavy, gasping breaths.

The West Marshal stood and slowly walked along the table toward her. "The Arcadia spider is unique among its species. It is one of the few predators in the world to go after prey that is often ten to a hundred times bigger than itself."

She stood over Dorothy and looked down at her. "How does it do this, you might ask? It injects a rather unique venom into its hapless victim, and then waits. As the venom spreads throughout the body, it begins to dissolve all the internal organs until they become a single pool of mush."

Dorothy tried to grab the West Marshal, but she knocked her easily back down. Dorothy sat down hard in the chair, her head drooping to one side. Spittle and foam forming at the corners of her mouth.

The West Marshal leaned in close. "That feeling you are experiencing right now. It's the feeling of melting."

Dorothy rolled her head to one side and looked one last time at Caleb. The fur around the corners of his eyes matted from the tears he could no longer contain.

The West Marshal grabbed her chin with a hand and twisted her head back. "No! You will look at me when you exhale your final breath."

Dorothy convulsed violently and heaved a final gasp before going limp in the West Marshal's hand, her eyes glazing over staring at nothing.

The West Marshal let her go and Dorothy pitched face first into a bowl of grapes.

Dead.

Chapter 2

Caleb stared at Dorothy lying face down on the banquet table. He had lied to Amanda when he said he tied the blue ribbon to the poisoned bottle. But that didn't matter when, just before they came into the banquet hall, she slipped the ribbons off both bottles and shuffled them quickly back and forth from one hand to the next.

"What are you doing?" He had asked her.

She continued shuffling the bottles back and forth until he no longer knew which one held the poison. "It's not like I don't trust you, because I don't, but I would rather let fate decide who died in there today."

He could not believe what he was hearing. "Fate?"

She shuffled the bottles even faster ensuring that neither one of them would know which was which. "Well, fate will decide for one of them. I will have to kill the other one myself."

He looked at her with his mouth open slightly in shock.

She smirked. "Don't look so surprised. My mother has grown weak and hides in her castle for fear that someone might try to kill her. She no longer deserves to rule over the Western Territories, let alone all of OZ. And don't get me started on your girlfriend. Nero informed me you might develop a soft spot for the girl, so he asked if I would be willing to let them both die and take over for my mother as the Queen of OZ." She winked at him. "Of course I would."

His heart beat so hard in his chest he thought it would burst right through his rib cage. His entire plan of poisoning the West Marshal for Nero and bringing Dorothy back alive was slipping out of his hands.

His eyes frantically tracked the bottles, but there was no way he could know which was which. He could only hope that fate was on his side and the West Marshal got the poisoned bottle.

That would give him time to save Dorothy.

Now, as he looked at her lying face down on the table, he knew fate was not on his side.

It was too late.

She had been the only person to treat him like anything other than a hybrid.

And now she was dead.

The West Marshal picked up Dorothy's hand and held it for a moment. She let go and the hand flopped back down to the table.

She spun around and smiled at Amanda. "You've done it, my dear."

Amanda stuck her chin out defiantly. "Was there any doubt Mother?"

The West Marshal continued to smile as she walked up to Amanda. "You've been disappointing me a lot lately. But it looks like you're finally turning yourself around."

"Disappointing you?"

The West Marshal placed a finger on Amanda's lips.

"Hush child. You are the daughter of the greatest ruler of OZ. You'll figure it out someday."

The West Marshal spun around and headed back to Dorothy's body. "It's time for me to claim what is rightfully mine."

Amanda's arm jerked violently out from under her cloak. "You mean what is rightfully mine!"

Caleb reacted on instinct when he saw the flash of steel as Amanda raised a dagger over her head and charged the West Marshal.

He sprang from a full stop to tackle Amanda in midair.

They both hit the ground hard in a tangle of arms and legs. The dagger skidded across the stone floor and the West Marshal caught it under her boot.

Caleb struggled with Amanda before finally hooking an arm under her neck and bending her back the wrong way.

She continued to struggle but it was no use. He was much stronger than she was and had his arms and legs wrapped around her like a squid battling a shark in the depths of the ocean.

The West Marshal plucked the dagger from the floor, walked over to Amanda and crouched down in front of her.

Caleb had Amanda on her belly. He pulled her head up so that she could look the West Marshal in the eye.

The West Marshal laughed. "What is it with kids these days? They feel entitled to a shortcut to power and success rather than doing all the hard work to earn it."

Her smile evaporated. "Let her watch me take the East Marshal's star."

She shifted her eyes to Caleb. "Then break her neck."

What was he doing? Why had he saved the West Marshal from Amanda? And why would he kill Amanda for the West Marshal?

Both of them had killed the only woman he ever loved.

His heart beat loudly in his chest.

That was why he had felt the way he did.

He loved Dorothy.

And he was certain she would have grown to love him.

He looked over at her lifeless form hunched over the banquet table.

His life was playing out like every fairytale he had read. It was always the same story. Two lovers find each other and one of them ends up dead before the other has a chance to say how he really feels.

The West Marshal yanked Dorothy's body back to a seated position and reached for the

Marshal Star pinned to the front of her leather corset. "I'll take that."

Dorothy's hand shot up and grabbed the West Marshal's wrist. "I don't think so."

The guards in the room screamed words like "sorcery" and "witch" before dropping their swords and bumping into each other trying to be the first out of the room. It did not matter how much they feared the West Marshal. Apparently, they feared the undead even more.

The West Marshal sucked in a sharp audible gasp.

Caleb slackened his grip on Amanda and she took that opportunity to stab him in the jaw with an elbow.

His vision flashed white momentarily and she wriggled free from his grasp. By the time he regained his senses and prepared himself to fend off Amanda's impending counter-attack he discovered that he, Dorothy and the West Marshal were the only ones left in the room.

And Dorothy was alive.

But if Dorothy was alive, than that meant…

He focused his attention on the West Marshal. Her face morphed suddenly from surprise to intense pain. Yellow foam formed around the corners of her mouth right before she hunched over and cried out in pain.

Dorothy twisted the West Marshal's arm while she stood, forcing the West Marshal down to the floor at her feet. "That experience you are having right now. It's you, melting."

The West Marshal tried to speak, but it came out only as a gurgling sound.

Dorothy tilted her head. "I'm sorry. Are you confused?"

The West Marshal's nod was nearly imperceptible.

Dorothy smiled. "During the short time I spent with Nero, he taught me a valuable lesson on how to stay alive. After I drank the water and you watched me so intently, I knew what you wanted. So I gave it to you."

The West Marshal looked up at her, her words came out in a hoarse whisper. "How?"

"How did I know I wasn't poisoned?"

The West Marshal nodded.

Dorothy looked over Caleb. "I didn't. But I figured if I was, there was little harm in pretending to die sooner."

The West Marshal's eyes glazed over and her arm went limp in Dorothy's hand. Dorothy grabbed the West Marshal's star from her corset before she let the lifeless body collapse on the floor.

Dorothy stood over the body of the West Marshal and looked at the tiny metallic star in her hand. It was so small and insignificant on its own, yet people had died to keep it. People had killed to get it.

What did not make sense were those who killed so others could have it.

She looked over at Caleb.

He shook his head as he stood up from the floor. "You were never the target."

"And yet you thought I was the one poisoned."

He walked slowly toward her. "Amanda switched the bottles around. I didn't know which bottle you would get."

"Why were you saying sorry as you came in here?"

He held his hands out, palm side up. "I didn't want you dying thinking that it was me who wanted you dead. That is the last thing I wanted."

She threw the West Marshal's star to the floor at his feet. "I think this is what you want."

Caleb looked down at it but did not pick it up. "No Dorothy…"

She yanked the East Marshal's star off her corset and threw it at him. "That's right, you wanted both of them."

It hit him in the chest and bounced to the floor, landing with a ringing clatter next to its twin. He bent down and picked them both up. "Nero wants these." He looked back up at her, the sadness in his heart reflected in his eyes. "I want something else."

She was sick and tired of Nero getting whatever he wanted and she wasn't about to let those sorrowful kitten eyes affect her judgment.

"Why do you help him? What does he have over you?"

"He does not have anything over me. He saved me as a baby and raised me as his own son. I owe him my life."

She shook her head. "You owe yourself the truth."

"What truth? You mean what Jetharo said?"

She nodded her head. "Yes. Don't you want to find out if Nero has been lying to you your entire life?"

"Of course I do. But first I have to get you somewhere safe."

"Why do you care what happens to me?"

"Because I'm in love with you."

All the anger and hatred she felt evaporated in an instant. "You... love me?"

"Ever since the day you beat down those thugs in that back alley."

"What am I supposed to do with that?"

"You do not have to do anything with that. But right now I have to get you somewhere safe." He held out the two Marshal stars to her. "And the safest place for you is behind these stars."

"And how are those going to protect me?"

"With these, you are the most powerful person in OZ."

"All that power won't get my father."

"We take these and give them to the Wizard…"

She interrupted him. "He's not the real wizard."

"He said he could find your father in exchange for the two Marshal stars. What does it matter who he really is if he can do that?"

She looked him square in the eyes. "I'm not going back there on his terms."

The door creaked open and her head snapped toward the sound. Two guards shuffled in and looked at the dead Marshal at her feet.

She grabbed the Marshal stars from Caleb and pinned them on her corset.

She stood up straight and cleared her throat. The two guards snapped to attention.

Her voice cracked a little when she started to speak but then she forced herself to sound commanding.

"I want you to bring Jetharo from the dungeon to me."

The first guard took a step forward and lowered his head. "The previous Marshal always visited him in the dungeon where she could remain safe with him behind locked bars."

"I am not the previous Marshal. Find Amanda and lock her up in the dungeon."

The guard clicked his heels. "As you wish."

The two guards pivoted on the balls of their feet and marched out of the room.

Caleb tilted his head and looked at her curiously. "What do you want with him?"

She let the breath out she had been holding and let her shoulders droop after the guards left the room. She took three deep breaths to calm her beating heart. "He knows OZ better than anyone. If anybody can help me find my father, he can."

"Do you think he'll help you?"

"I sure hope so."

"And what if he doesn't?"

"Nobody else can help me."

Caleb looked at the floor. "There is another way."

She tilted her head to the side. "If you know of another way, tell me."

He looked back at her, his face serious. "The phony Wizard still thinks that I am with Nero. I could take the two Marshal stars to him and get him to confirm whether Nero has your father or not."

"Won't he expect you to give him the Marshal stars?"

"I would have to take you with me as my prisoner. He would be too suspicious if you willingly gave up both stars. It would be better if he believed you were already subjugated."

"You think you can convince him that you tricked me?"

"I can be very convincing when I need to."

She heard a scuffle outside the door right before it opened and Jetharo was shoved inside. He muttered a few choice words under his breath as the guard ignored him and closed the door.

"What is the meaning of…" At that same moment, he saw the West Marshal dead on the floor. He looked up at Dorothy. "Oh. I see. There's a new marshal in town."

"How well did you know my father?"

"He and I were going to escape together. I guess I knew him as well as anybody could know him."

"Right before she died, the West Marshal told me that Nero has my father."

He nodded his head. "That's possible."

"Can you help me get him back?"

He regarded her for a moment. "Tell you what. There is something I need from my castle. If you go and get it for me, I can help you get your father."

Dorothy nodded. "We can help you get back into your castle…"

He cut her off. "I don't need to get in. You just need to bring something out."

Caleb leaned in and said, "Can I speak to you over here for moment?"

She let him lead her over to a corner and he whispered so Jetharo would not overhear them.

"I do not like this. Everybody wants you to do something for them in exchange for their help."

"I don't know what else to do, Caleb. If he can help me get my father, I'm willing to do anything."

His eyes darkened. "Are you willing to risk your life?"

"I'm willing to do whatever I have to, to find my father."

He leaned in close, but his voice was raised well above a whisper. "It is a fool's errand. We would need an army to storm his castle. Not to mention that we still need to go after Nero. It is not possible. We can find another way."

"What if I get you your army?"

Caleb laughed. "You wouldn't be able to convince any of the people here to go up against the Wizard's castle. It was designed to keep him in. It's also very good at keeping everyone out."

There was a knock at the door. Dorothy raised her voice to be heard through the closed door. "Come."

The door opened and a guard sheepishly shuffled in, his eyes cast down toward the floor. "It appears that Amanda has escaped in the airship."

Caleb quickly responded. "Which way was she headed?"

The guard looked up at him, apparently happy he was not addressing the Marshal directly. "She was pointed to the Southeast."

Caleb looked back at Dorothy. "She's going to Nero's casino."

Dorothy furrowed her brow. "How do you know?"

"There's nothing else in that direction."

"There is something else in that direction."

It was Caleb's turn to furrow his brow. "What else is in that direction?"

She smiled. "Your army."

She walked back over to Jetharo. "This thing you want, is it something I can carry?"

He smiled. "Oh yes. It will fit in your pocket."

She glanced over at Caleb, who did not look pleased. "Then it's settled. I will build your army, we will get what you want out of that castle and you will help me rescue my father."

Chapter 3

Caleb had been right. The safest place for her was behind the Marshal stars. They put her in charge and everyone around her immediately obeyed her every command.

After convincing Jetharo that she could help him take back his castle, she had commandeered the second-fastest airship in all of OZ.

Apparently, Amanda had taken the fastest.

Dorothy stared out the window of the airship's gondola. The expanse of OZ spread out below her from horizon to horizon. She should be thinking about many things.

Finding her father.

Defeating Nero.

Becoming ruler of OZ.

Instead, her thoughts kept returning to what Caleb said when they were alone in the banquet hall.

His words had cooled the fires of hatred she felt toward him and toward everything that came between her and her father.

She quickly realized she felt safe when she was with Caleb. Moreover, she believed him when he said he would stick by her side no matter what.

Nevertheless, she did not come to OZ to find love.

She came to find her father.

As much as she wanted to find her father as soon as possible, they were not headed for Center City or Nero's casino just yet. Even though she felt she held all the cards, Nero still possibly held her father. She would have to gather an army before she confronted Nero.

Not just any army would do.

She needed an army of brave warriors.

And she knew exactly where to find them.

The bravest person she had met in OZ was Munch. He had given his life to help her. All she needed to do was convince his clones that they were exactly like the original in more ways than one.

Caleb approached from behind and stood next to her. "I don't think you should be storming the gates of the Wizard's castle."

"I have to get the clockwork key for Jetharo from the royal chamber. The Wizard's not going to let us just walk in and start poking around for a loose stone in the wall."

"Do not forget, he sent you to kill the West Marshal and bring back her star. He's expecting us to just walk back in."

She turned to him. "But I don't think he would let us walk right back out."

He continued to look out the window and refused to make eye contact with her. "He would if he thought you were my prisoner and I was taking you back to Nero."

"And why would he do that?"

"He made a deal with Nero. He could stay there as long as he kept looking for this clockwork key."

She let in a sharp breath. "Nero knows about the key?"

"Nero knows a lot about the secrets of OZ. From what I have heard, that key unlocks the biggest secret of them all. And Nero wants whatever that key unlocks more than anything else in this world."

She narrowed her eyes at him. "I'm not giving Nero the clockwork key."

He turned fully to look her squarely in the eyes. "Do not worry about my loyalty. Nero lied to me about my family and my people. I no longer have any allegiance to him."

He turned away and stared silently out the window for a moment before adding, "Amanda will have reached Nero by now. If he has your father, like the West Marshal said, we need to contact him to negotiate a trade before he can do anything to him. That is of course, if the West Marshal was telling the truth."

She continued to look out the window. "She thought she was about to kill me. I don't see any reason why she would lie."

"I could think of a hundred reasons."

"Like what?"

"You, of all people, should have realized by now that people lie more than they speak the truth in OZ."

She turned to face him. "What about you Caleb? Have you lied to me more than you told me the truth?"

His eyes softened. "I'm not proud of that. But I am telling you the truth from this point forward." He gave her a playful smile. "And that's the truth."

She wanted to smile back but instead returned her attention to the window. What she first thought were storm clouds on the horizon half an hour ago had turned into dark broiling clouds that seemed to emanate from the ground. She gasped audibly when she realized the pitch-black clouds were actually plumes of smoke from the fires that raged throughout the city they were approaching.

The city that was their destination.

Munch's city.

They landed the airship beside a pile of rubble that used to be the wall that kept Munch and his kin safe from the outside world.

Dorothy's heart pounded furiously in her chest as she clambered over the rubble. Her heart skipped a beat when she saw what remained of the city.

Broken bodies and broken buildings were scattered everywhere like toys in a child's playroom. The tears in her eyes from the acrid smoke mingled with the tears from the pain she felt deep in her soul.

All of this was because of her.

A tiny voice called out to her from close by. "Marshal?"

She looked around and spotted the tiny figure trapped under a collapsed wall.

She rushed over and started pulling chunks of broken rock off him. "Hold still, I'll get you out of there."

Relief washed over his face. "I knew you would come. I told them Munch would bring you back to protect us. Some of my brothers doubted, but I never did."

Caleb joined her and together they pulled the rubble off the clone of Munch. When he was clear, Caleb lifted him up. The clone tried to stand but his face wrinkled with pain and he collapsed to the ground.

He looked up at Dorothy. "I think my leg is broken."

Caleb fashioned a splint from the surrounding debris and supported the clone to a standing position.

More cries for help drew their attention and they spent the next three hours pulling more clones from piles of rubble.

Soon there was a small ragtag group of clones gathered around her and Caleb.

The first clone they had saved looked around at the rest of the clones and then back at Dorothy. "Where's Munch?"

She looked at him without blinking. Slowly, she looked at all the clones as they waited for her response.

How could she tell this man the very person that gave him life, gave them all life, was dead?

Caleb cleared his throat and spoke for her. "I am sorry to be the bearer of bad news. Munch died saving Dorothy's life."

The little man smiled even though sadness was written everywhere else on his face. "I knew he could be brave. I am the one that finally convinced him to go to you, you know. I'm glad to know he died a hero. But it is sad to know that we will all die with him."

Dorothy was taken aback by this last comment. "What do you mean you will all die with him?"

The clone looked up at her, sadness reflected in his eyes. "The lifespan of a clone is 2 to 3 years." He waved his arms around him at what remained of the burned-out city. "And that is the best case scenario. We have a machine that can transfer our thoughts from one clone body to another, but without any new bodies for us to move to…" His voice trailed off into silence.

Another clone stepped closer and continued where his brother left off. "It takes about six hours to make a fully grown clone. But we need a clean sample from the original for every clone. We've tried to make a clone from a clone, but the results were…"

He glanced around him at the other clones before looking back at Dorothy. "Less than satisfactory."

She looked around at all the tiny faces who knew their days were numbered and then back to the leader of the small ragtag group. "Can you take a sample from me?"

The clone shook his head. "No. Munch was unique. He was genetically modified to be the perfect original for the cloning process. Without him, we are all doomed."

Her entire plan of convincing the two hundred clones in Munch's city to follow in the brave footsteps of the original evaporated like mist on a warm summer morning.

There were no less than a handful of battered and bruised clones left alive after the brutal attack. Not enough to form an army and take back the Wizard's castle before challenging Nero.

She had only one choice if she ever wanted to see her father again.

She unpinned the Marshal stars from her corset and turned to Caleb.

She held out the two stars to him. "I guess we'll go with your plan."

Chapter 4

The man who had become the Wizard with Nero's help stood on his balcony overlooking Center City and watched as the airship descended to the airfield.

Nero had told him he would put him in power as long as he located a simple little item for him. He often wondered if Nero would eliminate him if he ever turned over what he had been asked to find.

Even after the airship disappeared from sight, he stood there silently for over an hour until he saw the carriage enter through the front gates of his castle. He looked out over Center City, an oasis in the midst of the cracked and brittle earth that stretched out to the horizon on all sides.

Soon he would control more than his eyes could see.

Soon he would control more than half of OZ.

All he had to do was promise Nero that he would keep looking for that which Nero sought.

One of the Wizard's many servants, dressed in a muted gray suit, opened the double doors and stepped out onto the balcony. "They have arrived." When the Wizard did not respond, the man bowed as he backed out through the doors and closed them again leaving the Wizard alone on the balcony with his thoughts.

As soon as he had both Marshal stars, he would have the resources to break free from Nero once and for all. He never needed Nero. It was just more convenient to let that sniveling fool think he could pull the strings from behind the scenes.

It had been so easy to manipulate Nero and use him get two of the four Marshal stars.

When he controlled half of OZ, he would send Nero back to his little gambling house and take over from there. Nero thought he held all the power, but staying behind the scenes only meant it would be easier to get rid of him.

The Wizard chuckled to himself as he contemplated the alliance that was nearly complete with the Northern Marshal. Moreover, with the Southern Marshal locked behind her impenetrable wall, the Wizard would control everything that mattered and Nero would no longer be needed.

But first, he would need to take care of the girl and her pet.

The Wizard strode through his royal chamber and locked the doors behind him as he left.

He strode into the front hall and frowned. He had expected to meet with Dorothy and Caleb, but not like this. Caleb had Dorothy bound in chains with a burlap sack over her head. He yanked roughly on her chains and made her stumble as they came up the steps into the front hall.

Caleb saw him approach and held out the two Marshal stars in the palm of his hand. "On behalf of Nero, I present to you sovereignty over the Eastern and Western territories."

The Wizard took the Marshal stars and nodded his head at Dorothy. "Why is she bound and hooded?"

Caleb tugged on the chains as he spoke forcing her down to one knee. "She didn't wish to relinquish her star willingly. She needed to be reminded who was in charge."

The Wizard narrowed his eyes to slits and regarded the little girl with a new sense of respect. If she was still willing to stand up to Nero after everything, maybe she had not outlived her usefulness after all. "Leave her with me."

Caleb glanced sideways at his captive for a moment. "Nero has other plans for the former East Marshal."

"Nero is not here now. As ruler of OZ, I command you to leave her."

Caleb took a step back. "Do not forget who's really in charge."

"I have not forgotten. It is you who do not realize whose castle you are in."

Caleb took another step back and pulled on the chains, taking Dorothy backward with him. "I must be going. Nero is expecting us back."

Caleb reached the door when the Wizard pointed at them. "Seize them both."

Guards descended on Caleb and Dorothy from all directions and grabbed them.

Caleb struggled against the guards who held him. "Nero kept his half of the bargain. He will be very upset you are not keeping yours."

The Wizard walked up to Dorothy and turned to look at Caleb. "Let him."

He returned his attention back to Dorothy and yanked the burlap sack off her head.

Only, it was not Dorothy.

He held the burlap sack his hand and waved it at Caleb. "What is this?"

Caleb only responded with a smile.

The Wizard moved in close. "Where is she?"

Dorothy counted silently to ten after she heard the Wizard leave and lock the doors. She pushed on the pressure plate that would make the wall slide sideways and let her enter the same royal chamber the Wizard had just left.

Jetharo told her where he hid the clockwork key. It was in a hollow stone only twenty feet to the left of the secret entrance.

She would be able to sneak in, open the hollow stone, retrieve the clockwork key and get out within the space of a minute. By the time the Wizard discovered the woman with Caleb was not Dorothy, she would be back outside the castle walls. The Wizard would not dare harm Caleb for fear of Nero's retaliation.

Her heart beat softly as she waited for the wall to slide open.

Several long seconds passed while nothing happened.

She pushed on the pressure plate again and heard the same click she had heard before.

Still nothing happened.

Her heartbeat grew louder and stronger.

She looked back and forth along the narrow passageway. She was exactly where Jetharo said she should be.

Maybe the mechanism was old and stiff from disuse.

She pressed her shoulder against the plate and pushed with all her might.

It clicked louder this time and she heard the grating sound of stone on stone as the wall slid away.

Light from the royal chamber spilled into the secret passageway and she breathed a sigh relief. All she had to do was find the hiding stone, get the key, and get out.

She counted out the twenty paces on the stone floor visually with her eyes, looked up, and found herself staring at a massive oak bookcase covering the entire length of the wall.

Not a single wall stone was exposed for twenty feet on either side.

Chapter 5

Dorothy stared at the massive bookshelves that covered the entire wall from floor to ceiling. Every shelf bowed slightly from the weight of heavy books.

She walked the twenty paces and stood right in front of the bookcase. Jetharo said that the stone was scratched on one corner so she could quickly find it, but failed to tell her where on the wall it was.

I guess he assumed the wall would still be exposed, and not blocked off, she thought.

Was it closer to the floor?

She looked down.

Or closer to the ceiling?

She looked up.

Whichever choice she made, if she chose wrong she ran the risk of someone, most likely the Wizard himself, discovering her before she found the key.

Might as well split the difference and start in the middle, she said to herself.

She began sliding dusty tomes off the shelf in front of her and laying them in a stack on the floor.

The Wizard's hot breath reeked of stale milk. This was not something Caleb wanted his keen senses to be subjected to for much longer.

He had hoped the threat of Nero's wrath would keep the Wizard from detaining him.

But he was wrong and the Wizard apparently had plans of his own that did not include Nero. His first instinct was to find some way to warn Nero, but then he remembered that he and Dorothy were going after Nero themselves.

The only thing he had to do right now was figure out a way to escape from the Wizard.

The Wizard leaned in closer until his face was mere inches from Caleb's. "Where is she?"

Caleb's eyes flicked upward for only a moment, but that was all the Wizard needed. He leaned back and tilted his head to the side, a surprised look on his face. "He told you about the key."

The Wizard walked around in a circle and then came back to face Caleb. "Did he tell you where it was?"

Caleb struggled against the guards who held him. "I don't know what you're talking about. I brought you the two Marshal stars but I was not about to give you Dorothy. That is why I brought in a decoy. Nero wants her and I didn't want to give you the opportunity to take her first."

The Wizard stamped his foot. "You're lying!"

The Wizard stared into his eyes and the features on his face shifted as if suddenly realizing something. The Wizard looked up at the ceiling in the direction of the tallest castle spire and then back at him. "She's already inside, isn't she?"

Caleb dropped lower, putting most of his weight onto the guards who were beginning to struggle to support him. As soon as his legs bent halfway, he sprang up and threw the guards off balance.

Caleb moved swiftly and recovered his own balance as the guards flew to the ground on either side of him.

The Wizard was faster and darted forward, kicking Caleb in the neck with an outstretched foot.

Caleb went down, gasping for air and clutching at his throbbing neck.

The guards clambered back to their feet and yanked Caleb to his knees.

The Wizard placed his hands behind his back and leaned in, his sour milk breath assaulting Caleb's keen sense of smell again.

"There's more where that came from. But I think I'll give your little girlfriend her share first."

He stood back up and nodded his head at the guards. "Lock him in the dungeon. I am going to my royal chamber. I do not wish to be disturbed."

Stacks of dusty old books stood in leaning towers all around Dorothy's feet. She stared at every stone that made up the wall behind the cleared out shelves.

None of them had a scratch on a corner to signify it was the hiding stone.

Time was running out.

She had to look faster if she hoped to find it before the Wizard returned.

She no longer had time to be careful and methodical.

She ran in front of the shelves sweeping her arm across them, spilling books onto the floor in haphazard piles.

As she unceremoniously cleared each shelf, she took a moment to inspect the newly exposed section of wall.

Nothing.

She clamored up onto the growing pile of books to reach the next shelf and started tossing books over her shoulder.

A big chunk of stone missing from the wall caught her eye.

She pushed more books out of her way and stared at the stone with a scratch in its corner that had widened out into a missing chunk of stone.

She had found it!

She dug her fingers in the crevice around the stone and felt it move slightly.

She wedged her fingers further into the crevice and slowly slid the stone out of the wall inch-by-inch.

As soon as the stone was free, her heart skipped a beat and a huge smile spread across her face.

She turned the hollow stone around and stared into an empty container carved from the stone.

The hollow stone was hollow.

And very much empty.

Someone cleared his throat behind her. She yelped in surprise and nearly fell down the shifting pile of books. By the chamber door, the Wizard held up a polished brass key by a silver chain that hung around his neck.

"Looking for this?"

She stared at him from the top of the book pile and tried to judge the distance while compensating for the unbalanced weight of the hollowed out stone.

His eyes flickered to the stone for a brief moment. "We both know you're not going to throw that at me."

She released her grip on the stone and let it tumble down the mountain of books. It broke apart into several pieces when it hit the floor.

He looked at the key in his hand. "Nero put me here for the sole purpose of finding this. I spent months searching the castle for it but to no avail. Surprisingly, a worker discovered it while installing my bookshelves. He tried to keep this discovery from me and paid the ultimate price."

He tucked the key back into the folds of his robe. "Whatever is behind the door that this key unlocks, Nero wants it desperately. Just in case the key wasn't discovered, he hired your father to build a weapon powerful enough to get through that door. He gave the Professor a unique power source that would make it the most powerful weapon in the world. And do you know what he did with it?"

Dorothy shook her head.

The Wizard laughed. "He took that power source and carved it into two heart-shaped pendants. When Nero heard about that, he was furious and sent men to collect your father and the emerald hearts; but he was too late. Your father had already given one of them away and, due to the carelessness of the collection team, he no longer had any leverage to get the Professor to tell him where it was."

Her heart beat wildly in her chest. "Carelessness!? They killed my mother!"

"And then lost you. Needless to say, the Professor wasn't talking. And without a power source the weapon was useless, so the pressure was back on me to find the key. I made a good show of using his men to help me tear up whole sections of the castle in a desperate attempt to find a key we never would. I had all the time in the world to build up enough influence to make a stand against Nero until you showed up."

He pointed at her as he continued. "You brought the second emerald heart into OZ. I am sure you took the one the West Marshal had and you're probably wearing them right now."

She instinctively reached to where they hung just out of sight beneath her leather corset.

The Wizard smiled knowingly. "Of course you are."

He studied her face for a long time before speaking again. "Who are you?"

She shifted her weight uncomfortably from one leg to the other on the stack of books. "I'm nobody."

The Wizard waggled a finger at her. "You are not as insignificant as you would like me to believe. Let us not forget, you conquered two of the four territories in OZ. Not bad for someone who only arrived here a few days ago. I can't give you your father, I don't know where he is, but I can give you the chance to walk away from all of this. You give me both pendants and I will put you on an airship pointed in any direction you wish. I won't bother you ever again and Nero won't bother you."

"Even if I take you at your word, how do you know Nero will leave me alone?"

"Because you won't have anything he needs."

She pulled the two emerald hearts out from under her corset. They glowed brightly in her hand. "If I give you these, you will let me go?"

"Of course."

"And Caleb?"

"Not Caleb."

"I'm not leaving here without Caleb."

"My offer expires in thirty seconds."

She had been studying his movements while they talked. He was stiff and sporadic and, she noted when he stumbled on a couple of the books on the floor, slightly clumsy.

While he was not old, he was certainly past the prime of youth. She immediately knew how she could get what she wanted and not give up everything. "I have a counter offer for you."

She slipped the necklaces over her head and placed them on the empty bookshelf next to her.

"We fight for it. You win; you get the emerald hearts, the key, Caleb, and me. I win; I get the emerald hearts, the key, Caleb, and that airship you promised."

He studied her for a long silent minute and then slipped the silver necklace over his head and placed the key on the other end of the empty bookshelf by the door.

He tilted his head from side to side, loosening up his neck muscles. He stripped off the long flowing Wizard robes leaving only pants that hugged the muscles of his strong legs.

His legs and arms flowed quickly and smoothly through several practiced and perfected martial arts forms before he half crouched in a fighting position and grinned at her fiendishly. "Winner takes all."

Chapter 6

Dorothy realized her error as she stared at the physique of her muscular opponent. The Wizard lacked even an ounce of fat. Her eyes darted to the key on the shelf. All she really needed was that key. If she could get him to circle around to the other side of the room, she could grab the key and make a run for the secret hallway.

She half slid, half fell down the stack of loose books until she was on solid ground. There was no way she was going to try to mount an attack, or properly defend herself, standing on loose books.

She started to circle around the edge of the room expecting him to mirror her movements. But he was not cooperating. Instead of circling away from her around the room, he approached her causing her to stop and retrace her steps until they were both back in the same positions they started.

He regarded her with a smirk. "I'm not letting you near that key."

She crouched slightly to keep her center of gravity low. "I won't make the first move."

"Funny, I was thinking the same thing. Tell you what, why don't we flip for it?"

Without taking his eyes off her, he took two steps over to his cloak crumpled on the floor, bent down and fished through the pockets.

He stood up and showed her an OZ Schilling. "Heads I attack you first, tails you attack me. Agreed?"

She nodded her head slightly.

He tossed the coin in the air and, as his eyes tracked it so he could catch it again, she sprang forward. She swept her arm in a knifing motion to deal a debilitating blow to his neck. She did not want to kill him. Just knock him down, grab the key and get out while giving herself enough time to get away before he recovered.

Without taking his eyes off the spinning coin, he grabbed her right wrist with his left hand before she made contact with him and effortlessly threw her to the ground. He held onto her wrist and twisted her shoulder as she went down.

Pain shot through her arm like a thousand needles.

He caught the coin in the palm of his right hand while twisting her arm even further. She writhed on the floor trying to find a position that did not hurt more than the one she was in.

She tried to stand up but he kicked her feet out from under her. Her arm would have snapped in half if he had not crouched as she fell back onto her side.

He slapped the coin on the floor in front of her and took his hand away.

"Will you look at that? You little fortuneteller, you. It's tails."

Gritting through the pain, she pulled on the arm he held in his iron grip, pulling him forward and slightly off balance. As soon as he shifted his feet to regain his balance, she shot forward and clamped her teeth down on the hand that held her wrist. Instead of letting go, like she had expected, he forced his hand further into her mouth stretching her jaw back open.

She squeezed her jaw tighter until her mouth filled with the rusted taste of his blood.

He punched her in the side of the face with his other hand. She involuntarily released her jaw and he ripped his hand out of her mouth before shoving her away.

She somersaulted several feet away before she rolled back to a standing position. She took a quick mental stock of the damage to her body. Her right arm tingled as if she had slept on it all night. She massaged her numb arm, trying to force the blood back into it.

The Wizard inspected the bite on his hand and shook his head. "It was my understanding you had martial arts training. And yet, you resort to the tactics of children."

The feeling was starting to return to her arm, but she needed more time. "I didn't come here to fight you. I did not come here to fight anyone. I just came for my father."

He chuckled. "The little lost child looking for her father. With everything you have done to destabilize OZ, I thought you had loftier goals."

She wiggled the fingers on her right hand as the tingling sensation dissipated. "Yeah well, story of my life, such as it is."

He casually leaned against the bookshelf. "The feeling starting to come back to that arm yet? If not, I am willing to wait. I want this to be a fair fight."

She stood up a little straighter and stopped massaging her arm. "Okay, I'm ready now."

"Are you sure? I don't want to rush you."

"No. I am fine. Besides, it's your turn."

He tilted his head to the side. "My turn?"

"I won the coin toss for the first attack, but I already used that up. Now it's your turn."

He pushed off from the bookshelf, rolled his shoulders and swung his arms around loosening his muscles. "Well then, get ready. Because here I…"

She charged at him before he finished his sentence hoping to catch him off guard, but his swift response showed anticipation for everything she did.

Every kick, hit and jab she tried to land on him was efficiently blocked.

He blocked and parried several hits as she drove him backward to the wall.

She never even saw the fist coming toward her face, it happened so fast.

When she regained her senses, she was on the floor on her hands and knees looking down at splatters of blood on the floor that were dripping from her cut lip.

The Wizard hopped on the balls of his feet in front of her. "If that's the best you've got, it's no wonder you haven't found your father."

Her foot found purchase in the crevice between two floor stones and she launched herself at him. She slammed into his midsection and wrapped her arms around him tightly trying to force him off balance.

He pummeled her sides and lower back in rapid succession with his fists, but she continued to drive him backward until they both slammed into the wall.

He gasped as the wind was knocked out of him. She lifted her head quickly and caught him in the chin, rocking his head back with the impact.

Now that he was stunned, it was time to get him down on the ground. She reached down, laced her fingers around the back of his knee, and lifted.

He brought his elbow down hard on her shoulder and her arm instantly went numb.

He slammed his arm into the side of her head and she sprawled out on the floor.

He stumbled back along the wall away from her while he shook his head. She tried to get up, but her one arm refused to respond and she fell face first back to the floor.

He grabbed handfuls of clothing and hauled her to her feet. He spun her around and used the increased momentum to throw her against a bookshelf.

The force of the impact rattled her teeth and sent books crashing down on her. She was back on the floor again, only this time, she was under a small pile of heavy books.

Despite all her training and constant sparring practice with Mr. Bart she realized, as she lay among the books, she was not going to win this fight.

Tears threatened the corners of her eyes as her inner voice chastised her for quitting. But she was not quitting, she told herself. She had been beaten. She looked over at the man who had beaten her. His eyes were blood red with rage.

He kicked books aside to get at her when he suddenly stopped.

He raised his hands above his head and turned toward the door.

She looked past him and saw Caleb standing in the doorway pointing a flintlock pistol at the Wizard.

"Your time is up Wizard. Guards, chain him and take him to the airship."

Guards flooded the room and grabbed the Wizard. He struggled against them. "Do not listen to him. I am your master. I am the Wizard! This is treason!"

His cries echoed down the hallway outside as the guards led him away. She suddenly felt every bruise and laceration in her exhausted body. The sharp corners of the books jabbed painfully into sore muscles all around her. Rather than try to move, she decided to wait for Caleb to dig her out.

As he lifted her off the pile of books, she looked around at the empty shelves. "The key."

"I have it," Caleb said. "And your emerald necklace, too."

She relaxed into his arms as he carried her to the roof of the castle and onto the waiting airship.

As soon as he placed her in the bed of the captain's quarters, he lifted the down comforter up to her chin and tucked her in.

"You must rest. I will wake you as soon as we get there. I want you to be able to personally hand Jetharo his key."

As he stood up, she reached a hand out and grasped his wrist. "Thank you, Caleb. I couldn't have done it without you."

"Don't thank me yet. We still have to find your father."

Chapter 7

Dorothy stood on the hill overlooking her family home. The deep Kansas sky was even bluer than she remembered. A gust of wind blew a stray lock of hair into her face. She pushed the soft curl away from her eyes as she watched the lone figure climb the hill to join her.

She watched his face as he took his place beside her, placed an arm around her shoulders and looked out over the expanse of the family farm.

"Someday, Dorothy, all of this will be yours. Your mother and I will be gone and you will be all grown up."

Tears streamed down her face. "I'm not ready for you to be gone. Not yet."

He turned and placed his hands on her shoulders. "Nobody's ever ready. You just have to be strong."

"I've missed you so much, Daddy."

He held her close in a tight hug. "I've missed you too, sweetheart."

The ground beneath them shook violently. She was knocked to the ground but quickly scrambled to her feet and looked around.

Her father was gone. "Daddy?"

She scanned the countryside for any sign of him, but she was completely alone. "Daddy?!"

Thunder boomed over the Kansas plains and she looked up quizzically into the clear blue sky. Wait! It was not completely clear.

A fireball streaked across the sky, getting closer every second. She gauged its trajectory and realized, with the skip of a heartbeat, it was going to hit her house.

She looked at her house and saw her father wave at her just before going inside and closing the door.

She had to get him out of there.

She had to save him.

She started running down the hill as fast as her feet would carry her.

The fiery ball streaked over her head so close she could feel the heat.

She was too late.

The fireball slammed into her home and it exploded outward, knocking her backward... and out of her dream.

She jerked awake as she tumbled out of bed and onto the floor of the airship.

Another explosion sent the airship tilting wildly to the side. She rolled across the floor along with half the objects in the room.

She scrambled back to her feet and headed out the door for the pilot's cabin. She figured that is where Caleb would be.

Two more explosions rocked the airship as she stumbled her way to the front.

Just as she burst through the cabin door, she saw Caleb yelling into the microphone of the wireless. "Repeat. We are on a peaceful mission carrying food and supplies to the needy. Cease-fire! Cease-fire!"

Ever since they had met, she had never seen a look on his face as he had now. He did not look panicked and still maintained absolute control over his emotions. Nevertheless, she knew him well enough to know when he was worried.

She leaned heavily against the door to keep from falling over as the ship bucked about and yelled over the explosions. "What's happening?"

He motioned out the front window, even though all she could see was black smoke. "Air Pirates. And I would lay down 10 to 1 odds these are the same ones who shot you down."

"What makes you say that?"

"We're near the area where you first entered OZ."

She looked at him with a shocked expression.

"What can we do?"

"The best we can do is beg for mercy. Something these guys are not really fond of giving."

Another explosion rocked the airship sideways.

Caleb gripped the microphone. "Repeat. We are on a peaceful mission."

Through the eardrum pounding explosions, she heard a faint buzzing sound. It sounded like a swarm of bees, only it was much louder and getting louder every second.

Another explosion boomed. Only this time, the airship did not rock from the impact. In addition, the explosion sounded further away.

Two more explosions took place at a distance.

Caleb leaned across the window and peered out. "Someone's attacking the Pirates."

Dorothy leaned over the pilot's chair and stared out the window with Caleb. Small airships that lacked a gas envelope to make them lighter than air were instead equipped with wings like birds and propellers mounted on the back. They buzzed around the pirate airship like flies bothering an old dog. But unlike the flies around a dog, when these pests flew over the pirate's airship, they dropped fireballs.

Soon, the pirate airship was engulfed in flames and losing altitude on its way to the ground.

One of the winged airships matched the speed of the Wizard's airship and came alongside the pilot's window. She looked into the small cockpit and thought she saw Munch. He waved at Dorothy and raised a microphone to his lips.

The wireless cackled to life. "This is Bain, a brother to Munch. We heard your distress call over the wireless and recognized you as a friend of the East Marshal. We thought you might like our assistance."

Caleb smiled and pressed the button on his microphone. "Your assistance was perfectly timed. Thank you." He glanced at Dorothy. "And the East Marshal thanks you."

She could see Bain smile through the cockpit window. "It is our pleasure and our duty to serve, but we have to hide these aero-planes before someone sees them. They are only prototypes and if anyone knew we had something like this, they would have burned our city to ash long before now."

Bain's aero-plane dropped out of sight. Dorothy tried to find any sign of them out the window.

Just as quickly as they had appeared, they were gone.

Caleb placed a hand on her shoulder. "It's over now. Let's get you back to bed."

"I can't sleep. Not after that."

"You still need your rest."

"I can rest later. I want to talk to the Wizard."

He shook his head. "That's not a good idea."

She held her hand out.

Caleb handed her the key to the cargo hold. "I should go in with you."

She cupped his fury face in her hands. "Thank you, but I need to speak with him alone. You need to stay here on the bridge and keep this ship on course."

"Are you sure you'll be okay?"

"I'll be fine."

"All right. But if he tries anything…"

"I know. You'll hear me from anywhere in the ship and come running to my rescue."

Chapter 8

Dorothy faced the locked door to the cargo hold and took three deep breaths to calm her nerves.

She raised the key to the keyhole and her hand shook so much, she had to use her other hand to steady it enough to get the key in the door.

She heard the ratcheting sound of brass scraping against brass as she slid the key into the lock. A sudden dread came over her.

What if he broke free of his restraints?

What if he was waiting just beside the door?

Would she survive this time if he managed to get his hands around her throat?

She twisted the key until she heard a click, and waited.

It was deathly silent on the other side of that door.

She took another deep breath and let it out slowly.

She pushed on the door and listened to the iron hinges squeal slowly in protest.

The door swung open and she saw the Wizard kneeling in the center of the empty cargo hold. His head was bowed and it looked like he could have been in the middle of prayers were it not for the chains that bound him to the floor by his wrists and neck.

With his head still bowed, his voice broke the silence, making her jump. "How does it feel to be lied to?"

She stepped into the room and closed the door.

"Let's start with your lies."

He lifted his head and looked at her. "Which one?"

"How about the one where you're not the Wizard?"

He laughed heartily as if she told him a joke while sharing a pint at the local pub. "I have been the Wizard for over a decade. And I was just about ready to break free from Nero's iron hold…"

He cut himself off before saying anything further and let out a big breath that morphed into a sigh. "Ahh, well, water under the bridge. I forgive you."

"I didn't come here for forgiveness. I came to offer you redemption."

He jerked on his chains as he half stood, startling her. "Being the Wizard has given me the opportunity to make enemies everywhere. There is no redemption you can offer me. There is no salvation for me at all."

He bowed his head and settled back down on his knees.

She waited until her heart stopped beating so hard.

"My father can help you."

He tilted his head up and folded his hands into his lap. "You never answered my question."

"What question?"

"How does it feel to be lied to?"

"I'm not sure I know what you mean."

"Where are we headed right now?"

She hesitated.

He lifted his arms as far as he could until the chains drew taut. "I'm bound to the floor by chains and I'm going to find out once we arrive anyway. I think it's safe to tell me where we are headed before we get there."

"We are going to the real Wizard so I can give him the key that belongs to him."

He laughed louder. "Let me ask that question another way, little girl. How does it feel to be lied to by Caleb?"

"Caleb hasn't lied to me."

"Are you sure about that?"

"Of course, I'm sure."

"Then tell me this. Does your true Wizard work for Nero?"

She frowned. "Absolutely not."

"Then, you have been lied to my dear." He nodded toward the window. "Take a look outside."

She walked cautiously over to the window and her mouth fell open.

They were nowhere near where Jetharo said to meet.

Instead, they were descending straight toward Nero's casino back in the middle of the Eastern Territories.

She glanced over at the Wizard. "Why did Caleb take us here?"

The Wizard looked away from her and toward the door. "Why don't you ask him yourself?"

She looked over at the door and saw Caleb pointing a revolver at her.

Chapter 9

Caleb tossed Dorothy a large brass key with one hand while keeping the revolver pointed at her with the other.

"Unlock the Wizard's chains."

She caught the key with one hand and stood perfectly still. "Why are you doing this Caleb? We had everything. We had both emerald hearts. We had the clockwork key. Why did you bring us back here?"

He held pistol steady. "The plan was always to give the emerald hearts to Nero."

"Why?"

He motioned toward the Wizard with his revolver. "Unlock the chains."

"And if I refuse?"

Darkness filtered into his eyes. "Please don't make me shoot you, Dorothy."

Dorothy let out a long breath and inserted the key into the lock.

As soon as the chains fell away, the Wizard grabbed Dorothy by the neck.

She clawed at his hand as he tightened his grip but it was no use, he was choking the life out of her and the smile on his face told her he was enjoying every second of it.

Caleb took a step forward. "Nero is upset enough with you for withholding the key from him for so long. If you take away his ability to punish Dorothy…"

The Wizard let Caleb's sentence hang in the air before finally letting her go. Dorothy collapsed to the ground, gasped for air and touched her bruised throat tenderly with her fingers.

Caleb lowered the revolver. "You can, however, bind her hands and deliver her to Nero."

Her breaths came in rasping gasps as she looked up at Caleb, letting the hatred flow into her heart. He turned away so he would not have to meet her eyes directly.

The Wizard yanked her roughly to her feet and wrapped one of the loose chains around her wrists.

Dorothy remained silent as they led her through the back hallways of the casino, partly because her throat still burned and partly because there was nothing she wanted to say to either of them.

What hurt most was Caleb's betrayal. She had not expected anything less from the Wizard, but she thought Caleb was on her side. He even professed his love for her.

Now she knew it was all a ruse to gain her trust.

And it had worked.

What a fool she had been. She let her guard down for the briefest of moments and he took full advantage of it.

She suppressed the tears that wanted to flow because her mother told her to always be strong. And she needed to be strong now more than ever.

The two guards stationed outside of Nero's office each opened their side of the double doors as the small group approached.

The Wizard shoved Dorothy inside ahead of him. She stumbled and almost fell as she staggered into the massive room.

Nero turned from the window that looked out over Little Roma and frowned. "What is this?"

The Wizard came up behind her and shoved her again. "I bring you a gift."

She stumbled but regained her balance quickly and stood facing Nero.

Nero looked at the Wizard. "Why is she all tied up?"

"She's my prisoner."

"She cannot be your prisoner because she works for me."

Dorothy could not keep the look of horror from crossing her face. "I do not."

Nero turned to her with a smile. "Don't you?"

"No."

"Let's take a look at the facts, shall we?" He held up a single finger as he spoke. "One, you brought the second emerald heart into OZ at my request. Don't look so surprised. Who do you think sent out that message in the first place?"

He continued ticking items off on his fingers. "Two, you killed the East Marshal, but I must admit, the Air Pirates played a small part in that one.

"Three, you killed the West Marshal, granted with a little help from Caleb.

"Four, you found the true Wizard. I have already received word that we picked him up right where he was waiting for you.

"Five, you helped me discover a traitor in my midst.

"Six, and probably the most significant, you found the key I have been searching for my entire life. And for that, I am eternally grateful to you, Dorothy."

She shook her head in disbelief. "You can't take credit for any of that. I made every decision myself and you weren't even there." She glanced over at Caleb. "Even when you had your spy with me, he never suggested anything. He went along with everything I said. How can you claim you were directing anything? I did everything of my own free will."

Nero laughed. "Only God gives you free will. Most people who work for me usually do not even realize it. Besides, there must always be a little flexibility in any plan for it to succeed, don't you agree?"

She breathed heavily, the hatred building quickly inside of her.

"You have done well for me, Dorothy." He nodded to the two guards stationed against one wall. "Untie her."

The guards approached from the side and unwound the chains from around her wrists. The chains fell loosely to her feet and she massaged her sore wrists.

The Wizard looked quizzically from Dorothy back to Nero. "What are you doing? She is the enemy."

Nero locked eyes with the Wizard. "She is not my enemy. My enemies are the ones who lie to me. Now, who in this room has lied to me lately?"

The Wizard turned to run but the two guards who had released Dorothy were already behind him. They grabbed him and held him in place.

Nero looked over at Caleb and smiled. "I believe you have something for me?"

Caleb walked over and handed the clockwork key to him along with both emerald hearts.

Nero pocketed the hearts and walked slowly up to the Wizard as he twisted the key around in his hands. "When were you going to tell me you had found my key?"

The Wizard stared at him, but remained silent.

Nero let a tiny laugh escape his lips. "Were you afraid that once I had the key, I would remove you as the Wizard?"

The Wizard shrugged his shoulders. "The thought had crossed my mind."

Nero shook his head in disgust. "How could you be so small minded? I do not care about you being the Wizard. If you had just done as I asked, you would have been the Wizard over all of OZ."

The Wizard looked dumbfounded. "You would have made me ruler over OZ in exchange for that little key?"

Nero inspected the key. "I would have made you ruler over the whole world in exchange for what this key unlocks."

He looked up from the key back to the Wizard. "You have caused a lot of people a lot of trouble by keeping this from me. But there is one person in particular you have caused immeasurable pain."

Nero spun around to face Dorothy. "You see? I am not your enemy. If he had given this to me when he first found it, I would not have needed to borrow your father, you would not have grown up an orphan and you most certainly would not be here now." He pointed to the Wizard. "He is the reason for your sad and lonely existence."

He moved in closer to Dorothy and spoke barely above a whisper. "How would you like him to suffer for everything he has done to you?"

She clenched her fists and gritted her teeth. "You caused me all this pain, not him. I would rather make you suffer for everything you did to me."

"If you were to choose between killing him or killing me, who would it be?"

Her heart beat steadily faster. "I know exactly who I would kill."

"Are you sure?"

Her eyes darkened as she let the hatred spill out of her heart and on to her face. "Yes."

He took a step back and mocked a hurt expression on his face. "But I can give you what you really want."

"How could you possibly know what I really want?"

Nero nodded to a guard who had been standing by a small door on the other side of the room. Despite everything that had taken place, the guard had not moved from his post. It was as if whatever he kept in that room was more important than anything else that had happened in this one.

The guard opened the door and in walked Dorothy's father.

Chapter 10

Nero enjoyed watching the volley of emotions fight for control over the muscles in her face as Dorothy watched her father walk into the room.

Professor Benjamin Gale's eyes scanned the room as he entered and, when they fell on Dorothy, he stopped abruptly mid-stride.

His face lit up briefly before it was replaced by confusion. "Dorothy?"

She bolted across the room toward him. "Daddy!"

Despite being as tall as he was, she launched herself in the air at him with her arms open wide. He caught her in a hug and they spun around.

She buried her head in his shoulder and the tears spilled out. "I thought I would never find you."

He held her tightly for a moment before holding her back at arm's-length and staring into her eyes. "What are you doing here?"

She did not bother to wipe the tears on her face. "We got your message."

"That message was for William. Not for you."

"I wasn't going to just sit around and wait. I couldn't."

His face saddened. "You should not have come."

Nero cleared his throat to get their attention. It was time to finish what he had started. "This little family reunion is very touching Professor, but that is not why you are here."

He held up the two glowing emerald hearts. "I believe you owe me a weapon."

Benjamin stood in front of Dorothy, as if that would protect her. "I will not do anything until my daughter is safely away from here."

Nero drew a pistol from inside his coat and pointed it at Benjamin. "You finish what you started or I will kill you where you stand."

Benjamin puffed out his chest in defiance. "If you kill me, you will never get your weapon."

Nero regarded the man before him and realized killing him would be meaningless if it meant a delay in getting the weapon he was promised. "While that is not entirely true, I understand the need of a father to protect his child."

Nero lowered his pistol.

Benjamin glanced at Dorothy for a moment and then fixed Nero with a solid stare. "Put my daughter on an airship bearing to the north."

Dorothy gripped her father's arm. "No. I'm not going anywhere without you."

He turned around and carefully removed his daughter's hand and held it between his own. "I have to stay here and finish what I was hired to do. Then, and only then, will I know you are safe."

More tears flowed down her face as she shook her head. "I'm not leaving you."

Benjamin grew more intense. "I'm not asking you, Dorothy, I'm telling you. Get out of here and get somewhere safe. Now that I know you are in OZ, I will find you again. I promise."

Caleb stepped forward. "I can make sure she gets away safely, Professor."

Benjamin looked at him. "Thank you very much." He looked back at Dorothy. "Go quickly, before Nero changes his mind."

Nero chuckled. "You know me so well, Professor. I suggest you do as he says little girl. I am known to be very fickle with my decisions."

Nero sighed heavily as he endured more hugs and more tears. He nodded his head rapidly at Caleb who finally got the message and took Dorothy out of the room.

As soon as they left the room, he held out the two emerald hearts to Benjamin. "It's time to get started."

Benjamin took the emeralds and walked over to the machine that stood by the window.

The Wizard, who had remained silent, finally dared to speak. "Why do you still need the weapon when you have the key?"

Nero turned to him with a smile. "The key has but one use. Granted, its one use is very significant to the world, but my emerald powered weapon can be used for a variety of purposes."

Caleb entered the room. "Her airship will depart in five minutes."

Benjamin glanced out the window and then turned to Nero. "This window does not face north. How do I know if she's really leaving or not?"

Caleb bowed slightly. "I anticipated the Professor would require proof and asked the captain to circle the casino once before continuing on his journey to the north."

Nero returned Caleb's bow with a nod of his head. "Thank you, Caleb."

He turned to Benjamin. "I trust that will be sufficient?"

Benjamin regarded him for moment and then nodded before continuing his work on the massive brass and iron contraption that stood taller than he did.

"What about me?" the Wizard asked.

Nero regarded the man who had betrayed him. The man who withheld the key to unlock the door to the secrets of the universe. The man who had withheld ultimate power from him.

He walked up to the Wizard and stood in front of him. "What do you think I should do with you?"

The Wizard smiled nervously. "Let me go?"

Nero laughed and pointed a finger at the Wizard. "You are wrong when you think you are of no more use to me." He looked at the guards on either side. "Let him go."

The guards looked each other and then back at him.

"I will not ask again."

The guards released the Wizard and took two steps backward to stand in front of the double doors.

Benjamin stood back from the contraption. "It's done."

Nero grinned at Benjamin. "Splendid."

He walked quickly up to the device and stared at it. "How do you turn it on?"

Benjamin pointed at a small knob set in the middle of a brass faceplate. "Push that knob."

Nero reached a finger out and pushed the button until it was flush with the faceplate. A nearly imperceptible hum emanated from the world's first coherent light emitting weapon. His eyes glistened with excitement.

He snapped his head toward Benjamin. "How do I aim it?"

"Look through the tube mounted along the top. Whatever you see through it will be destroyed by the beam when you push that button there."

"How about a little demonstration, Professor?"

Benjamin looked around and then pointed at a bowl of fruit sitting on the edge of the table. "Swivel it around on its base until you can see that bowl of fruit on the table there through the tube. When you push the button, you will see what it does."

Nero gripped the two handles mounted on the side and swiveled the contraption around until he could see the fruit through the tube.

He pushed the button and there was a single deep thumping noise that he felt more than heard. The bowl of fruit exploded into dust.

Nero could feel the adrenaline coursing through his veins. "You have done well, Professor. But what does this do against flesh?"

Benjamin stammered as he spoke. "I designed this so you could get through a door. Not to use it against people."

"And that is why the scientists are not in charge of ruling the world. They just don't think big enough."

Nero swung the weapon toward the Wizard and pushed the button. "Like I said, I can definitely find a use for you."

The Wizard hunched over in pain and screamed right before every cell of his body exploded into dust.

Nero nodded his head in appreciation of his new toy. "What's the biggest thing this can destroy?"

Benjamin scratched nervously at his chin. "I'm not sure. Conceivably, if you turn it up all the way with that dial you could destroy an entire section of castle wall."

Nero glanced out the window and saw a new target. He looked back at Benjamin.

"Could this destroy an entire airship?"

Benjamin's eyes grew wide. "You promised to let her go."

"I did let her go. If you don't believe me, look for yourself." He pointed out the window. "There she is."

He grabbed the dual handles and swung the weapon around until it pointed out the window. He sighted down the tube at the airship hanging peacefully in the sky and pushed the button.

"Stop!" Benjamin yelled as the two guards sprang into action and grabbed him before he reached Nero.

Nero waited for a long moment and then pushed the button again.

The machine felt warmer, but the airship still hung in the sky in one piece.

He let out a loud exasperated breath and faced Benjamin, who struggled against the guards. "You promised me a powerful weapon."

Caleb took a step forward. "He mentioned you can increase the power with that dial."

He regarded the dial that had tick lines with numbers increasing from 1 to 10 around it. The dial was currently set on one.

He shrugged. "I guess I should listen better."

He twisted the dial all the way to ten and sighted down the tube. As soon as he found the airship again, he pushed the button.

The airship exploded in a fireball before evaporating into dust.

Nero's face broke into a wide smile. "You have served me well, Professor."

Benjamin stood still, no emotion played on his face. "And you have failed me, Nero."

Nero felt surprise at the bold comment. "I… have failed you?"

"I gave you but one task, to let my daughter go. And you failed. Now you will suffer the consequences of your actions."

Multiple explosions echoed in through the window.

Nero spun around and saw flames leaping up all around the city.

His city.

Strange flying machines dropped balls of flame into his city that erupted into massive explosions.

His city!

He could not believe that anyone dared challenge him. He spun back toward Benjamin. "What is this?!"

Benjamin smiled. "I believe it's called a rebellion."

"And who would be foolish enough to lead a rebellion against me? You?"

Benjamin shook his head. "No. Not me."

"Then who?"

Benjamin pointed to his left.

Nero's eyes followed the direction Benjamin indicated and his mouth fell open.

Dorothy stood in the open doorway, pointing a revolver at him.

"Me."

Chapter 11

Nero should have realized that introducing a new element in the delicate ecosystem that was OZ brought with it the possibility for unexpected results. Nevertheless, he thought his plan had enough flexibility to account for everything.

Gunfire joined the explosions outside the window as his army retaliated against the flying machines dropping their fiery bombs.

He looked quickly toward his guards who stood stiffly at attention and did nothing about Dorothy pointing a gun at him.

Who could have turned his own guards against him?

Who indeed?

He turned and looked at Caleb, who stood with his arms crossed over his chest. He returned his icy stare with a wry smile.

"What did she say to you to make you turn against me?"

"The truth."

"And you think I have been lying to you all this time?"

"You kept me from my people. You kept me from my parents."

"Do you know how the rest of OZ treats hybrids? Of course you don't, because I saved you from all of that. I saved you from a life of misery and pain."

"And what kind of life did you give me in return? You trained me from birth to be your warrior. To do all the things you did not want to do yourself."

Caleb looked at his furry-clawed fingers. He looked up from his hands to Nero. "You made me kill for you."

He sprang forward and Nero barely had time to flinch before Caleb wrapped his hands around Nero's throat and dug his claws into the flesh of his neck.

"I will no longer do your dirty work."

Nero resisted letting any of the pain he felt register on his face. "Have you told your little girlfriend how much you loved it? The thrill of the hunt? The pleasure of the kill? I barely had to ask before your victim was dead at your feet. You were the perfect assassin."

"I didn't have a choice."

"You always had a choice. I didn't keep you here with chains or threat."

"You made me your slave."

"I made you my son."

The claws dug deeper into his neck and Caleb frothed at the mouth. "You are not my father!"

Now that Caleb was blinded by rage, Nero could make his move.

He snatched the revolver from Caleb's belt and shoved him away. Before Caleb even hit the floor, Nero fired two rounds at Dorothy.

As fast as he was, Benjamin was faster.

He shielded Dorothy with his own body and took both rounds to his back, collapsing into her arms.

Nero ducked behind the weapon and checked the revolver. After the two shots at Dorothy, he still had four rounds left.

He peeked around the edge of the weapon and saw Dorothy kneeling on the floor over her father. She was ignoring everything else in the room except him.

Nero smiled to himself. This was all too easy.

He stood up quickly and sighted the revolver on the kneeling Dorothy. A gunshot resounded in the room followed by hot searing pain in his right shoulder that drove him back behind the weapon.

Caleb called out from behind a newly overturned table. "There's nowhere for you to go, Nero. Give up."

He looked at his bleeding shoulder as his arm went numb.

He lost the ability to use his right hand, his dominant hand. He gripped the revolver awkwardly with his left hand, unsure if he would be able to hit anything at a distance. His target would have to be big, close and not moving.

Nero glanced out the window. It appeared, he thought with a twisted sense of humor, he had selected the wrong name for himself.

Just like his namesake, he watched helplessly as his city burned.

But unlike his namesake, he was not mentally disturbed. He could still do something about this situation. Nero had but one chance to topple Dorothy's little rebellion before it took hold and spread across the populace of OZ.

Even if he had to sacrifice himself, it would be worth it.

Nero stood and moved closer to the window, the explosions increased with frequency while the return gunfire was more sporadic and less determined. "There is one place left for me. And I'm taking you all there with me."

He lifted the revolver and fired all four rounds into the delicate workings of the weapon.

He laughed aloud as he watched everyone scramble and rush for the door as the high-pitched whine increased in intensity from the self-destructing weapon. All the stored energy in the two emerald hearts was about to be released in a single explosion.

Nero shielded his eyes as the explosion evaporated his clothing and ignited every inch of his skin. Then the concussive wave hit and he watched the entire room crumble to pieces around his enemies as he flew out the window.

His last remaining thought as he formed his own streaking fireball to earth was that he had eradicated the blight he had foolishly brought to the land of OZ.

Dorothy held her dying father in her arms. Someone yanked hard on her arm and pulled her quickly to her feet. She was about to fight back when she realized it was Caleb pulling her at a full run away from an enlarging fireball.

They ran hand-in-hand just ahead of the shock wave that shook apart the casino. She glanced back once more and saw the stone floor crumble away as it swallowed her father. If they slowed down for even a moment, they would be swallowed by the collapsing floor as well.

Caleb had grown up in the casino and knew the layout of the entire complex like the back of his hand.

Which was good for her. While Caleb dragged her through the casino, a tear ran down her cheek as she relived her final conversation with her father.

He had looked up at her. "Are you unharmed?"

She knelt over him. "I'm okay."

He felt like a real person even though wires and metal shards protruded from his wounds.

The automaton at her feet bled and gasped like a dying human. "I am sorry I failed you, Dorothy."

She smiled down at him and stroked his face. "That's not true. You saved me."

He looked up at her, a deep sorrow mirrored in his eyes. "With this metal body I know I am not your real father. But I remember being your father. I love you and miss you so much Dorothy."

The tears welled up in the corner of Dorothy's eyes and spilled down her cheeks.

"I love you too Daddy. I will not stop looking for you."

Her father smiled up at her. "I am glad to hear that."

An explosion showered her in debris and forced her back to reality as they dashed out through a side exit just before the entire multistory building collapsed inward on itself.

They dove for cover as bits of marble blew outward. Dorothy felt searing pain streak across her cheek.

She rubbed her hand across her face and it came away smeared with blood.

Caleb picked her up and peered out through the choking dust that surrounded them in all directions.

They were literally out of the frying pan and into the fire.

All around them, the city was in flames. Massive decorative columns toppled over, crashing into the street and spraying huge boulders of marble in every direction from the impact.

They were not safe yet.

They had to get out of the city or the cut on her face would be the least of her problems.

She clung desperately to Caleb's hand as he led them through a crisscross pattern through the city.

Each time they turned down a path, they were stopped short by fires or collapsing buildings.

A few times, they were almost crushed by walls that waited to crumble until they were just underneath. Caleb's keen animal senses quickened his reaction time and he pulled her to safety away from death's outstretched hand each time.

Soon, they were climbing the hill that overlooked Little Roma.

They paused at the top and watched the fires spread to consume every part of the city.

Chapter 12

Dorothy inspected herself in the mirror and lightly touched the nearly healed scar that ran across her cheek. It was the only visible reminder of her narrow escape from the collapsing casino several weeks prior.

A voice interrupted her introspection. "Makes you look tough."

She jumped and spun around to see Caleb leaning against the door frame, smiling at her. He was dressed in a black silk suit and held a matching black top hat in his hand. He tugged with a finger at the heavily starched white shirt that pressed into the fur of his neck.

"I will never understand the human fascination with clothing that keeps you from being able to breathe."

Dorothy stood and let her own ornate silk ball gown flow around her to the floor. "Yeah well, try wearing a corset sometime."

Caleb pushed off the door frame with his shoulder and took a step toward her. "You do realize I am completely covered in fur and don't need to wear anything."

She frowned at him and placed her hands on her hips, or at least as close as her bustle would allow, and did her best to sound condescending. "You do realize, you are not a wild animal. There is still some civility in you and with that comes a certain responsibility toward prudence when in the company of a lady."

His face went serious and he stood up straight as he glanced quickly around the room. "My apologies, I thought you were alone."

She snatched the powder puff off the dressing table and threw it at him. He caught the powder puff in the air with one hand, but still ended up with a face full of powder as it erupted in a cloud of white talcum upon impact.

He coughed and sputtered as Jasper stepped around him into the room. "And that's why I let you go in ahead of me."

Caleb ruffled talcum powder out of his fur with a hand. "You knew she was going to do that?"

Jasper smiled. "No, but it gets us one step closer to even."

Caleb let out a sigh. "I couldn't let you warn her or it would have jeopardized the entire plan."

Jasper jutted out his bottom lip and put on his best pouting face. "You could've just told me rather than have the Wizard throw me down in the deepest dungeon."

Caleb laughed. "There wasn't time. Besides I got you back out as soon as it was over."

Dorothy stepped between them. "Boys, boys, boys. All the fighting is over. OZ is at peace now. We are fifteen minutes away from crowning the new king."

Jasper threw his hands in the air. "Yeah, about that, whose bright idea was it to make a robot the ruler of OZ?"

Dorothy stared him down. "My father. He built the first all-electric automaton in secret and programmed him to run OZ like a country rather than a prison. Nero took my father before he could put it in place. William knew about the plan and, when he found out my father was here, he brought the automaton with him on the airship. After we crashed, Munch found him and, thinking he had no programming at all, called him a scarecrow."

Jasper interrupted her. "And the rest is, as they say, history. I still think it's a bad idea."

A new voice entered the conversation from the doorway. "It's actually the best idea ever."

They all turned toward the door as Jetharo walked into the room. "A robot is not bound by the same wants and desires as a human." He nodded his head at Caleb. "Or animal. That makes him incorruptible. And that is exactly what OZ needs right now as it works toward becoming a nation of people and not a prison of inmates."

Jasper shook his head. "The world is not going to stop treating us like criminals just because we formed a government with an incorruptible robot as our leader."

Jetharo smiled at the boy. "I didn't say it was going to be easy."

He looked at the rest of the group. "I need everyone to take your places, the coronation is about to begin."

As they all headed toward the door, Jetharo touched Dorothy on the elbow. "I would like to speak with you alone for a moment."

He waited until everyone left and looked deeply into her eyes. "I can't convince you to stay a little longer?"

She placed her hand on his. "My father is out there. I can't waste another day without looking for him."

Jetharo's face grew somber. "We have been unable to establish contact with the Southern Marshal. I cannot guarantee what kind of reception you will get after you go over the wall. I wish you would reconsider letting us send you with an armed escort."

"Caleb thinks, and I agree with him, that we will not be seen as a threat if it is just the two of us."

He paused as if wrestling with two conflicting ideas in his head that battled fiercely until one of them defeated the other. He let out a sigh. "Since I cannot change your mind; I have a request, can you do something for me?"

"Of course. Anything."

He reached into his pocket and produced the clockwork key. "I need you to take this with you and bury it somewhere in the Southern Territories. Never tell anyone, not even me, where you hid it."

She took the key from him and stared at it. "What does this key unlock?"

"Even though Pandora's Box is just a Greek myth, this might as well be the key to that box." He gripped both her arms with a strength that belied his age. "Promise me that you will bury this key where no one can find it."

She looked into his eyes and saw only sadness. "I promise."

Chapter 13

Scarecrow stood in front of the throne with the Woodsman at his side.

Attendees, lucky enough to secure a ticket to be inside the coronation hall, were packed so tightly everyone had to alternate breathing since there was not enough room for them to all take a deep breath at the same time.

The massive crowd spilled out of the Wizard's Castle and into the streets of the surrounding town. Despite this being the largest gathering of people in one place at the same time in OZ, it was completely silent. Even small children understood the importance of why they were here and did not run around through the crowd as they usually did.

The eerie silence in the coronation hall was broken by a single clear voice as the Wizard Jetharo raised the crown into the air.

"When you accept this crown, you pledge your loyalty to every individual in OZ."

Scarecrow bowed his head forward and allowed Jetharo to place it on his head.

Scarecrow's amplified voice echoed through the hall. "I pledge to put the needs of the people of OZ before my own and wear this crown for them."

The crowd erupted with excitement that quickly spilled out into the street.

The coronation ceremony lasted less than five minutes, but the ensuing coronation festival stretched on for three months as the royal entourage traveled from city to city to give every individual in OZ a chance to personally meet their new king.

Dorothy and Caleb joined the entourage for the first week until it passed within twenty kilometers of the wall that separated the Southern Territories from the rest of OZ.

They traveled on foot the rest of the way until they stood at the base of a wall hundreds of feet high made from the strongest ceramic modern science could produce.

There was no way they could break through it. In addition, the base was buried another several hundred feet below the ground, so tunneling was also not an option.

They would have to go over it.

Caleb dropped his backpack to the ground and pulled four suction cups with leather straps on them from his backpack. He tied two of them to Dorothy's knees. "These can support most of your weight but they don't have the grip of the handholds."

He reached into his backpack and extracted two more suction cups, each with a handhold attached to it. He slammed the suction cup against the side of the highly polished ceramic wall and it stuck. He hung from it to verify that it would support his entire weight and then pushed the release button, popping the suction cup back off the wall.

"These are going to keep us from falling off the wall, but remember to use the knee supports to bear some of the weight or your arms will tire too quickly."

She nodded as she craned her neck back and tried to see the top of the wall.

He pulled another complete set out of his backpack and strapped on the knee supports before he donned his backpack and slapped both suction cups against the wall.

He looked over at Dorothy. "Are you ready?"

She gave him a wry smile and slapped her own two suction cups against the wall. "Last one to the other side catches and cooks dinner."

Chapter 14

Scarecrow sat on the throne lost in deep thought. Without the need to breathe, he looked more like the statue of a king on a throne than the actual king of OZ.

A knock echoed across the throne room.

Scarecrow stirred to life. "Come."

The doors opened and the Chief Investigator of his Royal Guard strode in. He cast a wary glance at the Woodsman, who stood near the throne ready to protect the king from any danger.

The man bowed and knelt as he approached the throne.

Scarecrow stood up. "What are your findings?"

The man looked up from his knelt position. "The entire grave site was desecrated. The seal on the sarcophagus was broken and the body was apparently searched."

Scarecrow stared past the Chief Investigator as if he was not even there. He hadn't even been king for six months when the Wizard Jetharo was tortured and killed. They hadn't been able to find a clue who had murderer him, and now his grave had been defiled.

The Chief Investigator cleared his throat. "It's as if they were looking for something they thought might have been buried with him."

Scarecrow paused for moment, more for effect than the need to think more on what he had already decided. "Repair the grave site and post a twenty-four hour guard on it. Find whoever is responsible and bring them to me. I will not let the death and desecration of the Wizard Jetharo be a blemish on this fledgling government. The people have to be shown that this type of behavior is no longer tolerated in OZ."

The Chief Investigator bowed his head once more. "Yes, your highness."

He stood up and walked backward out of the throne room in a half bow, the doors closing behind him.

A voice echoed from behind the throne. "You are wasting your time on things that do not matter."

Scarecrow turned around quickly and saw a man dressed in a full-length cloak, a hood hiding his head and face. "Who are you? How did you get in here?"

The cloaked figure pulled back his hood to reveal his hairless head and deeply scarred skin.

Despite the burns over his entire face and head, Scarecrow recognized him immediately. "Nero."

He turned to the Woodsman and pointed at Nero. "Kill him where he stands!"

The Woodsman spun up his chainsaws and charged across the throne room toward Nero.

Nero stood his ground, as if he knew there was no point in running.

As the Woodsman got closer, he raised both chainsaws high into the air ready to slice Nero in half. As soon as he reached him, the Woodsman froze, his chainsaws ground to a halt and he stood as still as a statue.

Nero removed a hand from his cloak and held up a small box with a single button on it. "You forgot I had this, didn't you?"

Scarecrow went to take a step and rid OZ of Nero himself when he realized his body refused to obey his mental commands. He tried to move his body, but he could only turn his head and look around.

Nero's face twitched as he limped slowly toward Scarecrow. The agony of the burnt and scarred skin that covered his entire body was evident on his face.

"You have the markings of being the greatest leader OZ will ever know. However, you lack one very important piece. You still need someone who is able to work behind the scenes to accomplish things that cannot be done in the public's eye. In essence, you need a man behind the curtain. Someone who will guide you. Someone who will give you counsel. Someone who will help you be better than great. I would like to be that man. Any objection?"

Nero paused as if waiting for one of the two automatons, under his complete control, to reject his idea.

Of course, they could not.

Nero bowed stiffly in front of Scarecrow. "I accept the appointment."

He stood back up and looked at Scarecrow as if he were an equal rather than the king of OZ.

"With the details of who is really in charge out of the way, it is time to focus on more important matters."

Nero shuffled closer to Scarecrow and looked him in the eyes.

"Where did Dorothy go with my key?"

Other Books by the Author

A is for Apprentice (Fantasy)

Oliver Twist: Victorian Vampire (Fantasy)

A Tale of Two Cities with Dragons (Fantasy)

Shade Infinity (Science Fiction Thriller)

Peacekeepers X-Alpha Series (Thriller)
    Inherit the Throne
    The Warrior's Code

Steampunk OZ Series (Science Fiction Serial)
    Forgotten Girl
    The Legacy's World
    Emerald Shadow
    The Future's Destiny
    The Dangerous Captive

Missing Legacy
Shadow of History
The Edge of the Hunter

Fugue: The Cure (Science Fiction Short Story)

Stay informed about all the trouble I keep getting into. Subscribe to Steve DeWinter's Book Report (i.e. the mailing list) @ SteveDW.com